D0439421

THE STORY OF WOLVERINE

Adapted by Thomas Macri

Illustrated by Val Semeiks and Hi-Fi Design

Based on the Marvel comic book series Wolverine

MARVEL

New York

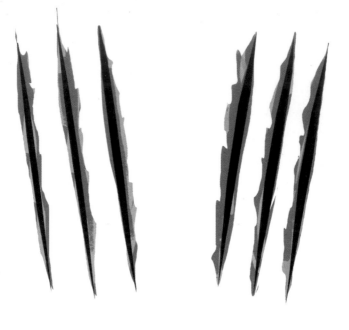

marvelkids.com

© MARVEL

Printed in the United States of America

First Edition

1 3 5 7 9 10 8 6 4 2

G658-7729-4-13121

ISBN 978-1-4231-7081-5

SUSTAINABLE FORESTRY INITIATIVE

Certified Chain of Custody
Promoting Sustainable Forestry

www.sfiprogram.org
SFI-01415

The SFI label applies to the text stock

James grew up in a big house.
It was in the mountains. He played
with his friends, Rose and Dog.

The kids grew up together.

When they were young they'd play tag.

As they got older they hiked and fished.

Dog and his father were poor.
James and his father were rich.
Dog and his father were jealous
and angry.

One night, the father and son
kicked in James's door.
They broke into his house.

Dog's father wanted to hurt James's father. James was frightened!

James's hands started to feel strange. He looked at them. He didn't know what was happening.

His hands started to shake.

Claws popped out of his hands!
He didn't know what to do.

James was in pain.
The claws hurt!

James's claws went back into his hands. The scars healed right away! He could not be hurt! People would think he was a freak. Rose had a plan to save him.

She grabbed his hand and they ran
as fast as they could.

They sneaked onto a train. They
were going to run far from home.
They'd go somewhere no one would
know them.

They arrived in a snowy place. They
met a man name Smitty. He was a miner.

James went to work for him.
He pushed carts full of coal.
He changed his name to Logan.
This would help him lay low.

Logan grew older. He never stopped
working hard.

He used an ax to chop lumber.

He hunted with a spear.

But most of all he loved being in
the wild. There he could use
his claws. It was the only place he
could truly be himself.

One day while Logan was having
dinner, two men came and
kidnapped him.

They hooked him up to machines.
The machines gave him metal claws!

Logan escaped from the lab.
He ran out into the snow.
It was so cold ice formed on his
metal claws.

He was saved by two Super Heroes.
They were called Vindicator
and Guardian.
They gave him a costume.
They gave him a Super Hero name.

They called him the Wolverine!

He became part of a team.
They were called Alpha Flight.

He also fought alone.

One of the first times he did this,

he fought the Hulk.

The two heroes locked in battle.
It was a very even fight.
Neither of them won.

Wolverine met the X-Men.

Professor X was their leader.

He told Wolverine that he was
a mutant.

The X-Men were mutants, too.

They were born with their powers.

Logan had always felt alone.
But now he knew others like him.
The X-Men were outsiders, too.

And with the X-Men, Wolverine had found a family.